Published by Modern Publishing,
a Division of Unisystems, Inc.

Copyright © 1986 Victoria House Publishing Ltd.

Designed for Modern Publishing by Victoria
House Publishing Ltd., 4–5 Lower Borough Walls,
Bath, England

® —Honey Bear Books is a trademark owned by
Honey Bear Productions Inc., and is registered in the
U.S. patent and trademark office.

Printed in Belgium

THE SQUEAKY LION

Written by Stewart Cowley
Illustrated by Colin Petty

MODERN PUBLISHING
A Division of Unisystems, Inc.
New York, New York 10022

Woollymane Lion was yellow and brown.
He was King of the Jungle and wore a gold crown.
Woollymane knew what lions were for;
They had to be proud, with a frightening roar!

But one night he dreamed a huge slithery snake
Came creeping to get him and he couldn't escape!
He ran and he growled until he was quite weak,
And what once was a roar, was now only a squeak!

The next day he crept down the old jungle track,
Trying and trying to get his roar back!
"Please stop!" said the Crocodile through a hedge,
"That terrible noise sets my teeth all on edge!"

So Woollymane Lion sat on the jungle floor,
And once again tried out his very best roar.
He tried it on four legs, he tried it on two,
But one tiny squeak was all he could do!

The animals gathered one by one,
To discuss Woollymane's problem and see what could be done.
Bobby Baboon waved his spoon in the air
And cried, "It just isn't fair!"

"What good is a king," said Jimmy Giraffe,
"Whose very best roar just makes people laugh?
Who will protect us? We're not safe anymore,
With a king who sounds like a rusty old door!"

"I'm supposed to be King of the Jungle!" Woollymane cried,
"But who will fear a lion that's all squeaky inside?"
He felt so ashamed, it was hard not to cry,
So he wandered away with a tear in his eye.

The animals stood watching in sad dismay,
That their wonderful king was wandering away.
They were all sure it was only a matter of time,
Before Woollymane got his roar back, and everything would be fine.

But deep in the jungle all was not well,
From the tall leafy trees rang a loud warning bell.
Far below a mean old snake slid out of the leaves,
He was grumpy and hungry and not easy to please.

That mean old snake looked all around
When the King of the Jungle couldn't be found.
"Well, I'm King of the Jungle now," the snake hissed,
"That silly old lion won't even be missed!"

The terrified animals huddled and hid
In a huge wooden box and pulled down the lid.
One tiny monkey peeked out and shivered with fear
As he watched the huge snake come much too near.

The monkey ducked back inside with a horrible shout,
"He's coiling around us to squeeze us all out!"
But they didn't know that help was in sight
Thanks to Percy the Parrot's brave, courageous flight.

"Quick, your majesty," cried the colorful bird,
"Your friends are in danger, or haven't you heard?"
"I shouldn't have left them," Woollymane thought, "I'm to blame!"
He crashed through the jungle like a runaway train!

The snake looked up in startled surprise
As Woollymane leaped out with pure rage in his eyes.
Woollymane puffed up his chest and he said,
"Stop bothering my friends, try to scare me instead!"

"Ha!" said the snake, "I'm not afraid of you!
I've heard that a tiny little squeak is all you can do!"
Then Woollymane got so angry that he let out a great roar,
And he blew the stripes off the snake, who was heard of no more!

Now the Lion that squeaked, doesn't squeak anymore.
The King of the Jungle now has a mighty loud roar.
He's more kingly and brave now, it certainly seems,
That he'll never be frightened again by a snake in his dreams!